Tom's

Robert Leeson says:

Robert Leeson was born in Cheshire in 1928. He served in the Army in the Middle East and worked abroad before returning to Britain, where he has been a journalist for over forty years. He is the author of seventy books for young people, as well as studies of industrial history and literary criticism for adults. In 1985 he was awarded the Eleanor Farjeon Award for services to children and literature. Robert Leeson is married with a son and daughter, and now lives in Hertfordshire.

Some other books by Robert Leeson

THE DOG WHO CHANGED THE WORLD
LIAR

For younger readers

GERALDINE GETS LUCKY
NEVER KISS FROGS!

ROBERT LEESON

TOM'S
WAR

PUFFIN BOOKS

PUFFIN BOOKS

Published by the Penguin Group
Penguin Books Ltd, 80 Strand, London WC2R 0RL, England
Penguin Putnam Inc., 375 Hudson Street, New York, New York 10014, USA
Penguin Books Australia Ltd, 250 Camberwell Road, Camberwell, Victoria 3124, Australia
Penguin Books Canada Ltd, 10 Alcorn Avenue, Toronto, Ontario, Canada M4V 3B2
Penguin Books India (P) Ltd, 11 Community Centre, Panchsheel Park, New Delhi – 110 017, India
Penguin Books (NZ) Ltd, Cnr Rosedale and Airborne Roads, Albany, Auckland, New Zealand
Penguin Books (South Africa) (Pty) Ltd, 24 Sturdee Avenue, Rosebank 2196, South Africa

Penguin Books Ltd, Registered Offices: 80 Strand, London WC2R 0RL, England

www.penguin. com

Tom's Private War first published 1998
Text copyright © Robert Leeson, 1998
Illustrations copyright © Kenny McKendry, 1998
Tom's War Patrol first published 2001
Text copyright © Robert Leeson, 2001
Illustrations copyright © Stephen Player, 2001

Published together as *Tom's War* 2003
1

Text copyright © Robert Leeson, 1998, 2001, 2003
Illustrations copyright © Kenny McKendry, 1998, 2003
Illustrations copyright © Stephen Player, 2001, 2003
All rights reserved

Made and printed in England by Clays Ltd, St Ives plc

British Library Cataloguing in Publication Data
A CIP catalogue record for this book is available from the British Library

ISBN 0–141–31544–X

Contents

Tom's Private War

ILLUSTRATED BY
KENNY MCKENDRY

For Thomas

1

TOM MET THE rest of the Orchard Road gang on the Meadows, as usual, that Saturday morning.

''Lo,' said Duggie. Molly grinned. William gave him a quick nod, then issued his orders.

'We'll go to Burley Wood, and do the jumps.' Without waiting for an answer, he set off down the path over the fields, outside Daneford.

Tom groaned to himself. In Burley Wood, the game was jumping across the stream, each leap getting bigger as the brook ran wider. Molly thought it a daft game and sat it out. Duggie did a few jumps then waded over, leaving Tom in unequal contest with William – usually landing short – in the water.

They walked in silence. The sun was hot, another scorcher, the last of a terrific summer. A smashing holiday was nearly over.

On Monday, Tom, Duggie and Molly started at the big school, three miles away, down the hill from Daneford, in Castlewick town. William had been there a year already. He was the expert. Nobody talked about school any more. William had said the last word on that subject.

Besides, something else was on their minds, something bigger, much bigger, but vague, like a cloud on the skyline.

They all knew this was the last weekend of peace. There was going to be a war. There was nothing else for it.

Tom felt a touch on his arm.

'What are you thinking about, Tommy?' asked Molly. 'The war?'

He made a face and nodded.

She nodded too, and put an arm round his shoulder. Ahead of them, William turned and glared.

'Get a move on, you lot. Last one in the wood's a sissie.'

He broke into a run down the slope. The others followed more slowly. Below them stretched open parkland. Beyond was Burley Wood, dark and green.

Then William pulled up so sharply the others almost ran into him.

'Look at that,' he yelled. 'Look at that!'

2

CROSS THE LEVEL turf of the park a fence now stretched, rough posts and wire. Behind it lay a sea of green and brown, not grass but row on row of tents. Among them moved hundreds of men in brown shirts and trousers.

By the fence a man in full uniform barred the way, rifle slung over his shoulder. The gang stopped open-mouthed.

'Hey, mister,' said Duggie. 'Can't we get

through here any more?'

'Don't be a dope,' snapped William. 'Course we can't. The Army's taken over. Come on.' He took charge once more. 'We'll go down the Clough.'

That was more like it, thought Tom. The Clough was a steep slope running down from the edge of the Rec to the canal bank. It was dotted with gorse bushes and the game was rolling downhill without getting full of prickles. No winners, no losers.

The gang faced about and headed back towards Daneford.

'Hey,' said Duggie, jerking his thumb back towards the camp. 'Do they have to live in those bell tents all the time? It's murder. I slept two nights in one with the Scouts. Freezing cold, earwigs down your neck, beetles up your bum . . .'

'Dah!' jeered William. 'They won't be here long. They'll be off over to France. My dad reckons it'll last six months, no more. When the Allies gang up on Adolf – you'll see.'

'I don't know,' said Tom. 'My dad says that's what they thought in the Great War. And he was in France for four years.'

William was crushing. 'Well, your dad doesn't know anything about this war. My dad does. He's an air-raid warden and he knows about all the secret weapons they've got.'

Tom stood his ground. 'My dad might be going in the Army again. He knows all about it.'

'Get off,' snorted William. 'He'll be too old.'

'They reckoned on the wireless,' put in Duggie, 'that all blokes'll have to go, right up to forty-one.'

Everyone was silent. Forty-one was old.

'They'll be taking women as well,' said Molly. 'I'm going to join the Land Army.'

'You never. You're not old enough,' came from William.

'I will be when I'm seventeen.'

'Come on,' said Tom. 'Let's get a move on before some other gang gets to the Clough.'

William didn't like anyone else giving orders. But the others were running already. He put on speed, passed them and ran on. Molly gave Tom a grin.

'Never happy unless he's in front,' she murmured out of the corner of her mouth.

Tom grinned back. Molly had her cousin sized up.

But William had stopped again, by the gateway to the Rec, waving for them to halt.

'Military objective, right ahead,' he shouted.

3

THE FAR CORNER of the Rec, beyond the football pitch and the swings, was ringed in with barbed wire, cutting off the way to the top of the Clough.

Inside the steel ring were more men in khaki, without jackets, sleeves rolled up. They were filling sandbags and building a wall round a deep, fresh-dug pit.

At the centre of the ring, grey steel barrel pointing skywards, was a gun, unlike anything

Tom had ever seen in the magazines about the Great War.

As the gang drew closer, a tall, sandy-haired soldier left the working party and came up to the barbed wire. He had a cheerful red face and blue eyes.

'Hey, mister,' said Tom. 'What's that gun?'

'Ack-ack, son.'

'What's ack-ack, mister?' asked Molly.

William turned on her. 'You are a dope. It's anti-aircraft.' He turned to the soldier. 'My dad's an air-raid warden.'

'Oh ah.' The soldier gave William a strange look.

'Hey, mister,' put in Duggie. 'What are those things on your sleeves? Are you an officer?'

The soldier laughed. 'No, son. Those are my stripes. I'm a bombardier.'

'That's the same as a corporal,' put in William knowingly.

Tom wanted to say, 'My dad was a bombardier in the last war,' but he kept it to himself. He didn't want to start William off again.

In any case, William had taken command. 'Right, you lot. Get lined up. We'll go up to the Croft.'

He saluted the soldier and the gang was marched away, leaving him shaking his head.

The Croft was a field on the other side of Daneford, with an oak tree where the gang often gathered at weekends. From its branches you could see for miles.

No sooner had they all climbed into their favourite seats than Duggie pointed. The other three followed his outstretched finger in amazement.

On the distant western skyline, glinting in the afternoon sun, swinging on invisible cables, were huge grey elephant shapes, twenty or more in an enormous circle.

'Airships,' gasped Duggie.

'Nah,' corrected William. 'They're barrage balloons. They're supposed to stop German bombers getting through to Liverpool and the docks.'

'Do you think there're really going to be air raids?'

'There's forced to be,' said William. 'Liverpool's going to be bombed flat, my dad said. And I'll tell you what. All the kids from Liverpool are going to be taken away.'

'Get off,' said the others in disbelief.

'Honest. They call them "evacuees". They'll be bringing some here.'

The gang was silent. Tom looked across the sky at the swinging grey elephant shapes. Yes, there was going to be a real war and it was coming here.

What Tom didn't know was that his own private war was about to begin.

4

ON SUNDAY, AT quarter past eleven, the war started, officially. Tom wasn't impressed at first. There was just this tired old man's voice on the wireless.

His dad looked out of the window and whistled through his teeth, as he always did when he was working things out. His mum put her apron up to her eyes. Tom felt strange inside.

He forgot about the war for a while when

he tried on the sports gear and school cap they'd just bought for him. He didn't have to wear full school uniform – the family couldn't afford it.

Then the war became real again. Tom took his gas mask out of its brown cardboard box. It was black, shaped like a pig's head, with a round plastic snout. Dad helped him on with it, fixing the straps at the back of his head.

The rubber smell was powerful. The perspex window misted up and Tom felt he was choking.

'Breath in and out steadily,' Dad said in his ear. The panicky feeling died, but he still couldn't see anything.

Dad pulled the mask off his head and they rubbed soap on the inside of the eyepiece. Then Tom pulled it on again himself, and he could see and breathe easily.

'Hey, can I go over to Duggie's with it on?' he asked.

'You can not.' His mum sounded angry. 'It's not a toy. You keep it safe in case it's needed some time.'

'That's it,' his dad chuckled. 'Wait till Bert Harris comes round with his rattle, shouting "Gas! Gas! Take cover!"'

'Frank, you ought to know better than joke about it.' Now Mum was telling Dad off.

Dad shrugged. 'Well, if I can't joke about it, who can?'

'I expect Mr Harris is only doing his duty,' went on Mum.

'Oh ah,' said Dad. 'But I can't stand him marching round like Lord Muck in his tin hat, as though the Germans are coming already.'

'Their William's just as bad as his dad – always throwing his weight about.' Tom had his say.

'You mind your own business – and get ready for Sunday School.' His mum put a stop to the argument.

When Tom got back later that afternoon, Mum and his sisters were cutting up big lengths of black cloth, while Dad fitted it to the kitchen window.

'Hope there's going to be enough blackout stuff,' she said, handing up another piece. 'You can't get it for love nor money now. There's queues at the shops for everything.'

'Ah,' muttered Dad through the safety-pins between his teeth. 'Queenie Robertson got in a queue for hair-grips and found she'd signed on for the old age pension.'

'Trust her,' began Mum, then burst out laughing. 'You're pulling my leg.'

'Anything's possible these days,' answered Dad. 'There.' He climbed down from the window. 'That'll have to do. We'll find out tonight if it lets light through.'

5

TOM LAY AWAKE. His younger brother in the other bed had dropped off already, but he was too excited to sleep. He could hear Mum and Dad moving about in the kitchen, locking up for the night.

He slipped from the bed and peered out of the window. Outside it was pitch dark, like a cellar. No moon, no street lamps, just a faint glow from the works in the valley below.

A terrific rat-tat-tat on the front door made him jump.

'Who's that?' He heard his mum's voice from the kitchen.

'I'm just going,' his dad replied. Bolts squeaked at the door below. Tom almost crept back to bed but curiosity kept him at the window. Faint movements from across the street told him there were other nosey parkers.

Now Dad had the front door open, speaking briskly. 'Yes, Bert, what can I do for you?'

'Mr Taylor.' Mr Harris's voice was very formal. Tom could hear where William got his way of talking from. 'I must ask you to put that light out.'

'Whatever for, Bert?'

'There's a distinct beam from your front window.'

'A little glim,' replied Dad. 'That's just

possible. We'd barely enough blackout cloth. Anyway, we're just off to bed. We'll fix it tomorrow. Good night then.'

'Tomorrow is not good enough. If you cannot adjust the curtain then the light must be extinguished.' Mr Harris became even more formal.

'I suppose they can see it all the way to Berlin.' Dad was sarcastic now. 'And they can't see the light from the works furnaces, eh?'

'They are not my responsibility. This street is, Mr Taylor, and I am ordering you to put that light out.'

'Oh, you are. Well, let me tell you, Air-raid Warden Harris, if you want to make me, you can fetch Sergeant Collins up from the police station to do it. Now good night.'

'Mr Taylor.' William's dad began to sound desperate. 'Don't you know there's a war on?'

'You what?' Dad's voice was sharp. 'I know more about war than you ever will.'

Across the road, a window went up with a slam. Then Tom heard Widow Robertson's screech.

'You tell him, Frank. Ask him about all those torch batteries he's keeping under the counter in that shop of his, till the price goes up.'

Air-raid Warden Harris couldn't face action on two fronts.

'You think on, Frank Taylor. I'll come back and check that window tomorrow.'

'You're welcome,' said Dad caustically. 'And good night.'

There was no answer, only the sound of retreating footsteps and windows quietly closing. The night was black and silent as Tom sneaked back to bed.

He was chuckling to himself over the way his dad had put William's dad in his place. But further down in his mind he had a sneaking feeling this might not turn out to be so funny.

And he was right.

6

AFTER THE NIGHT'S excitement, Tom overslept. Or he would have done if his mother hadn't turned him out of bed. She made him eat his breakfast properly, though, and he just caught the school bus at the top of Orchard Road by the skin of his teeth.

It was full already, but Duggie had saved him a few inches of space to squash into at the front. As Tom climbed on board, there was silence, then someone further along the bus started to whisper. By the time the bus was trundling down the hill, there were sniggers and chuckles.

Duggie nudged him. 'Hey, d'you hear that? It was all over the place this morning.'

'What was?'

'Who are you trying to kid? Your dad tearing a strip off William's last night.'

Tom sneaked a look behind him along the crowded seats of the bus, then turned round

just as quickly. William sat there, his face stony.

Oh no, thought Tom.

But last night's rumpus vanished from his mind as the bus rolled into Castlewick, and Duggie and he jumped down to join the long trail of kids trudging up the road to school. Both carried their bags over one shoulder and gas mask cases on string across the other. They wore their new caps on the back of

their heads, as the bigger lads did. When they came near the school gates they could twitch them down to the correct angle over their eyes.

On the opposite pavement walked a crocodile of girls, Molly among them. Tom would have liked to wave but didn't dare. From now on boys and girls were kept apart for lessons and in separate playgrounds. They had to wait until evening or the weekends to get together.

Behind him Tom could hear William's voice. There was some pushing and shoving going on among his classmates. Duggie nudged Tom.

'Let's get a move on. They leg the new lads over if they can get up close.'

They speeded up. Tom noticed that the whole column was marching faster as the new boys tried to keep out of range. The school gates came into view and the stride

became a trot. Finally they went through into the school yard at a gallop, to the derisive laughter of the older lads.

The morning passed. They were shunted from one room to another until they settled in their own form. But Tom's relief did not last more than a minute.

Their teacher, a huge man with a bullet head and short-cropped hair, marched in.

'Gas,' he bellowed. 'One, two, three.'

Tom reached under his desk for the cardboard box and scrabbled with the lid. In vain . . . it would not open.

'Six, seven, eight . . . '

Desperately, Tom turned the case round. The lid stayed shut.

'Nine, ten. That boy in the corner is dead.'

From round the classroom came honking noises as the other lads laughed inside their gas masks. The teacher loomed over Tom.

'Give it to me, lad.' There was a ripping sound. 'Some smart alec thought it a good idea to put sticky tape on this boy's gas mask case. That could be lethal . . . lethal!'

From the back of the class, a boy blew into his mask. The air escaped from the rubber rim with a farting sound.

'You,' yelled the master. 'Outside. Class! Masks off and away.'

For the rest of the day, till the joke palled, Tom was asked if he wanted to be buried or cremated. But it was bearable, and by the time Duggie and he were heading for the terminus, he could laugh at it himself.

As they boarded the bus for home, they saw William with his mates.

''Lo, William,' they called.

''Lo, Duggie,' answered William, deliberately. But he looked past Tom without a word.

7

THAT WEEKEND THE 'vaccies' arrived from Liverpool – a coachload of them, pale and miserable, clutching cardboard suitcases, name labels tied to their coats.

Tom's mum was sorry for them. She wanted to take in a boy or girl but the house was too crowded. Widow Robertson, though, was on her own. She took an evacuee and the whole street knew about it.

'It's a crying shame. Those snobs up Birch

Lane looked the poor jiggers up and down and picked out the cleanest ones. When it was all done this poor little chap was left.'

Poor little chap? He was the same age as Tom, but hard as nails, Tom could see that, with a face like a ferret, a sharp nose and red eyes. He came out into the street just as the gang met up. William, who seemed to be in a good mood again, winked and raised his voice.

'Yeah, you know where Liverpool is – that little place across the Mersey from New Brighton.'

The evacuee rose to the bait.

'It's on the map, any road, not like this dump. There's nothing here, no flicks, two shops, a load of fields and a bunch of useless cows.'

'Our cows aren't useless,' said William, loftily.

'What use are they?'

'They give good milk, that's what.'

The Liverpool lad stared in disbelief.

'Don't be gormless. You don't get milk from those mucky things. It comes clean in bottles, round our way.'

The gang burst into laughter, punching each other. Even Molly, who felt sorry for him, had to grin.

The pale face reddened. He picked on Tom, who was his own size.

'What are you laughing at?'

Tom choked, and said hastily: 'Nowt, mate.'

'It had better be nowt, kidder.' The evacuee's tone was menacing. He turned on his heels and went into Widow Robertson's entry.

William looked scornfully at Tom. 'Fancy letting a Scouser talk to you like that. You should've poked him one.'

'Oh, forget it,' said Molly hastily.

But William was not going to forget.

8

SOME JOKER — TOM never found out who — started a new craze at school. They sneaked up behind the victim and cut the string on their gas mask case, sending it down to the ground with a clatter, then disappearing into the crowd.

That morning they picked on Scouser — as the Liverpool lad was now known.

And who was there, just a yard away, trying to keep a straight face when Scouser's gas mask case fell down? It was Tom.

Scouser lunged forward: 'You did that, you rotten git.'

'I never,' protested Tom.

Scouser raised his fist. William appeared out of thin air.

'No scrapping where the teachers can see. Over by the lavs.'

Like magic a crowd had gathered. Scouser and Tom were swept across the yard to a corner, safe from prying eyes, and in no time a circle formed.

'Get on with it, do him!' urged William. Reluctantly Tom put up his fists. But Scouser was on the move already, and using a different rule book.

Lowering his head, he ran it full into Tom's stomach. As Tom doubled up, Scouser caught him a beauty on the nose with his fist.

Before Tom could lay a finger on his opponent, the whistles sounded. The crowd streamed away, Scouser triumphant among them.

'You were useless,' William told Tom, who was dabbing his injured nose. 'You have to get him one back. You can't let a Scouser do that to you.'

'How can I?' demanded Tom. 'He doesn't fight fair.'

'Well, we won't either.'

'How d'you mean?'

'You leave that to me,' said William mysteriously, and turned his back on Tom.

9

DAY BY DAY, after his clash with Scouser, the sinking feeling grew in Tom's stomach. He wanted his own back, yet he couldn't start another fight just like that. How did he know what Scouser would do?

What made it worse was seeing the evacuee every day in the street or the school yard with his mates. He would call out cheerfully: 'How's your nose, kidder?'

Even worse, Duggie sniggered the first

time it happened, until Tom sent him a withering look.

But suddenly, Scouser stopped his needling. Maybe he had tired of it, since Tom pretended to ignore him.

On the other hand, maybe something else was on his mind. By Wednesday that impudent smirk had gone from the pale face.

'Hey,' said Duggie, 'what have you done to Scouser? He looks sick – sort of scared of you.'

It was a comforting thought, but Tom didn't believe it. Scouser didn't scare that easily. What was going on?

On Thursday Tom found out. William appeared on his doorstep after school. Without a 'Hello', he began. 'Right, it's all fixed, for Saturday.'

'What's fixed?' Tom was bewildered.

'Getting your own back on Scouser, you dope. I promised you, didn't I?'

'Ho-ow?' Tom was uneasy at the gleam in William's eye.

'The Caves. I challenged Scouser. You both go down in the Caves and the one who stays in longest, wins.'

Tom's heart dropped into his boots. No one went into the Caves. At the foot of the Clough, near the canal bank, was a dark tunnel leading to abandoned salt-mine workings. Years before, the earth had collapsed in the lower galleries, letting in canal water and closing the mines. But at ground level, deep inside the Clough, a small maze of dank tunnels was still open.

'You're mad,' gasped Tom. 'If we go in there we might never come out again.'

'Yeah,' said William with relish. 'You should've seen Scouser's face when I told him. But he couldn't back out. He'll be there

Saturday morning with his mates. So you get your own back. OK?'

Friday evening came and another caller. It was Molly.

She whispered, 'Got something to tell you, Tommy.'

Tom called back into the kitchen, 'Just

going up the road, Mum. Won't be long.'

As they reached the street, Molly said, 'Listen Tommy. This Caves thing. William's trying to get you.'

'Me?' Tom's voice rose.

'Hey, be quiet. Yeah. After what happened last Sunday over the blackout. Your dad made a monkey out of his dad. William wants his own back. He couldn't care less about Scouser. It's you he's after.'

'Get away,' said Tom, but he knew Molly was right. William never gave up on a grudge.

'Look, Tommy. Why not tell Scouser it's quits? He's just as scared.'

'Can't do that.' Tom's mouth clamped shut on the words.

'Well, look.' Molly quietly passed Tom a slender metal object. 'Take my fountain pen torch I had last birthday. No one'll spot it, but it'll help you in the Caves.'

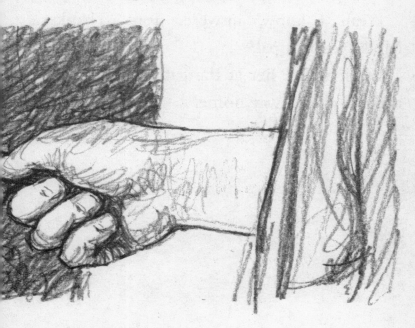

Tom shook his head. 'Can't do that, Molly. That'd be cheating.'

'Tom, don't be daft. If you fall down the borehole in the dark, what'll that be?' She nudged him and slipped the flashlight into his pocket.

Now they were in the top lane, Molly slipped her arm into Tom's.

'Look, William's my cousin, but he's so bossy I get fed up with him.'

'Yeah, I know,' answered Tom. 'Thanks, Molly, you're a pal.'

Later he left her at the gate of her house and ran all the way home.

10

WHEN TOM REACHED the canal
bank on Saturday morning,
Molly, Duggie and William were
waiting, but no one else was in sight.

'Hey up,' he said. 'Maybe he's too scared to
come.'

But just as he spoke, Scouser, white-faced
and scowling, appeared round a bend in the
towpath. Behind him were two mates, as
tough-looking as he.

Scouser halted, pointing at the steep bank

of the Clough reaching high above them.

'Look at that. The tunnel's boarded up. We can't get in.'

Tom's spirits rose. Scouser was as scared as he was. And for another thing he was right. The opening to the mine workings was blocked with old railway sleepers.

But before he could say, carelessly, 'Well, that puts the tin lid on it,' William strode up to the bank, took hold of one of the timber baulks and jerked it aside. A dark slit opened in the green hillside and from it came a foul smell of cellars and drains.

'Got your gas mask, kidder,' joked one of the Liverpool lads. But neither Scouser nor Tom were laughing.

'We'll never get in there,' protested Scouser.

Faking boldness, Tom stepped forward. 'Want to give in, kidder?' he jeered.

'Up yours,' answered Scouser charmingly.

William raised a hand. 'Our man goes first. You follow. We keep time outside. After ten minutes we call you out. The one who gives up, or skrikes for help before that, is a sissie. OK?'

'OK!' Tom and Scouser spoke together.

'Now.' William spoke to Scouser's mates.

'Let's synchronize our watches.'

'What watches?' said one evacuee sarcastically, lifting his bare arm.

'OK, we'll manage on mine then,' answered William pompously — just like his dad. 'In you go, Taylor.'

Duggie moved up alongside Tom. 'I'll hold that other plank back — give him more room.' Then he whispered to Tom: 'Listen, mate. My brother says inside on the right, twenty yards, there's a side tunnel. Hide in there till he gives up. Good luck.'

'Thanks, Duggie,' Tom whispered back, and holding his breath tight, he thrust himself through the gap into the foul emptiness beyond.

11

WITH EVERY STEP Tom took the cleft narrowed, until he found himself gripped on both sides. All around was dark, pitch blackness, darker than any night, blacker than the blackout. It was as though the whole weight of the Clough was squeezing him, tighter and tighter.

A squealing sound burst on his ears. His heart leapt. Then he realized it was the sound of his own breath forcing its way out.

He drew in a great lungful, then regretted it. The stench of dead air, trapped under the earth for years, was horrible. Gritting his teeth, he took shallow breaths, one, two, three, and began to advance into the void. One breath, one step.

The rough sides of the passage, part soil, part rotting timber, plucked at him. The air was harsh in his throat. But he had to go on. Breath, pace, breath, pace.

Twenty. His right arm shot into space. Duggie's brother was right. There was a side vent. Carefully he turned right, twisted his body round, backing into the opening.

It was all by touch – he could hear nothing, see nothing. He began to feel dizzy. Lights flashed in his eyes.

He'd stopped breathing. His chest felt as if it would burst. Start again, in, out, one, two.

William had said ten minutes. Ten minutes

was ten times sixty seconds, six hundred altogether. He would count to six hundred and then go out. They couldn't crib at that.

As he reached fifty, a sound from the tunnel beyond his hiding place shook him — a slithering sound like a snake, a giant snake. It came closer. Tom went rigid, his skin crawling.

Then, from the darkness, only a few feet away, came a ripe Liverpudlian oath. Tom choked on a hysterical laugh. It was Scouser. If he reached out from his hiding place, he could touch him as he went past. But Tom kept still, hardly breathing. If he was going to win this dare, Scouser had to believe that Tom had gone further in, where he daren't follow.

Suddenly light flashed on the roof of the outer passage. Scouser had a torch! He was cheating. He was even more scared than Tom.

For a second the light swung into the side gallery. Tom ducked but the beam wavered back. Then it vanished as Scouser pressed on into the darkness.

As he went he muttered. 'I won't . . . give up. I won't let those . . . Danefords . . . beat me.'

The sound died away. Tom's sides ached with silent laughter, his chest with held breath, his head with relief.

12

TOM'S BODY GAVE a great jump. His mind had gone blank. Had he fallen asleep? Maybe he was dreaming. He wasn't in this dark foul-smelling hole under the earth. He was in his bed at home and soon he'd wake up.

He put out a hand. He could feel the soft slimy soil of the walls, the chill creeping up his legs. He was in the Caves. And so was Scouser, somewhere in the darkness.

How long? He'd lost count. He thought

quickly. Say two hundred. He began again. Two hundred and one, two hundred and two. No, that was too slow. One, two, three . . .

The voice in his mind chanted monotonously and his thoughts wandered again. Did blokes used to work down below, under the canal, with their lanterns, chopping at the rock salt, all day, every day? Were they down here when the water burst in? Did they drown?

Ninety-nine. He came back to reality. Was that three hundred or four hundred? He tried to concentrate but the numbers hypnotized him. He beat on his leg with one hand – forty-six, forty-seven . . .

At last he could stand it no longer. It was six hundred seconds – ten minutes. Time was up. It had to be. His legs were so stiff they hurt as he lurched forward, hands waving in front of him.

In the main cutting he halted. There was not a sound from Scouser, wherever he was, not a gleam from that cheating torch.

A stray thought struck him. Maybe Scouser had sneaked back to the open air. If so, I've won. The notion gave him fresh strength, and he pushed boldly ahead till the closing walls told him he was at the entrance.

He could see the opening now. Thrusting and wriggling, he tumbled out into the daylight, the brightness hurting his eyes.

He gazed around him. No one there. They'd gone, the rotten lot. No, wait a bit. He could hear voices, laughter. They were having a giggle about him.

The sounds came from behind a bush some ten yards away. Dropping to his knees, Tom crawled up to it. Then raising his head, he heard a clicking sound. Someone was playing cobs.

He sprang up, ready to tell them what he

thought of the lot of them, then ducked
down again. There were five there – William,
Molly, Duggie and two Liverpool lads. No
Scouser.

Molly spoke. 'William. We ought to look
for them. It's well gone ten minutes. I
counted.'

'Get away.' William spoke carelessly.

'Nowhere near. Let's have another game. OK, kidder?'

A spasm of anger shook Tom. William had set this up. He didn't give a toss, though, what happened to Scouser or to him.

Then came a spasm of alarm. If Scouser were still down there in the Caves, the Liverpool lad had won. Wait a bit, though. No one up here knew that and neither did Scouser. He could sneak back inside, hide in the side tunnel and wait for Scouser to give up.

Then came a spasm of deeper alarm. Real fear. Suppose Scouser hadn't come out because something had gone wrong.

Turning and clenching his teeth, Tom fought his way back, past the timbers, into the dark tunnel once more.

13

TOM BURST THROUGH into the wider space beyond the entrance, ran, tripped, fell. The earth was slimy. Spitting, he struggled up and on. Where was the side turning? He'd forgotten to count and he was past it already.

Dope! He'd forgotten something else. He had Molly's torch. Fumbling, fingers greasy with mud, he fished it from his pocket and pressed the switch.

A narrow jet of light made the roof glisten.

Then it showed up the darker darkness of his hiding place. He plunged in, waving the flashlight ahead of him.

There was no way through, just a cave-like space. Back to the main tunnel he went, and pressed on. Darkness and silence wrapped around him.

'Scouser!' he yelled. His voice died in the

great emptiness. 'Scouser! You there?' He tried again. 'It's well gone ten minutes!'

No answer. That was wrong. He had to be there. A sudden terrible thought stopped Tom's rush. Maybe the Liverpool lad didn't know about the lower galleries, or the shaft that led down to them. Maybe he'd fallen . . .

The tiny torch beam circled the ground, then the roof. Nothing. Nothing.

'Scouser!' The sound echoed back to Tom as he moved into a much larger space.

The earth beneath him crumbled. He slipped and slid. Then his knees jarred against something solid. The torch clashed on metal.

Soil and stones loosened by his feet flew away. Heart in mouth, he heard them splash into water far below.

The torch went out. The bulb must have broken when it hit the iron rails. Fearfully, Tom reached out and felt a grid shape in front of him. Then his hand slipped into nothingness. There was a hole in the grating.

Scouser had fallen through.

For seconds he clung to the iron grille, then slowly he forced himself to go back the way he had come. He had to get help.

Even as he turned he felt something touch his shoulder and his neck. With a half scream he swung and struck out with all his might.

14

HIS FIST HIT something hard and soft in one. A light shone in his eyes. A voice cried out in pain.

'Aaargh! Me nose!'

'Scouser!' yelled Tom, in relief. 'Where have you been? I thought you'd fallen down the borehole.'

'I thought *you* had,' came the amazed reply. 'I've been looking for you.'

'Get away.' Tom started to laugh. 'How's your nose?'

'How d'you think, kidder? You got your own back, eh?'

'Yeah,' said Tom. 'It's a draw.' Then he remembered. 'You know, I thought you'd gone out so I went to look. That lot out there are playing cobs. We could have drowned for all they cared.'

'Right, mate. But you came back to look for me?' Scouser sounded incredulous.

'Course I did,' said Tom. 'I mean, you

wouldn't have been down here if we hadn't . . . ' Then he had another thought. 'Where were you hiding?'

Scouser grabbed him by the arm. 'Come on, kidder, I'll show you. There's another hole.'

'There's lots.'

'This is different. Come on.' He dragged Tom behind him, his torch beam lighting the way. They were in another, narrower, passage.

Tom could feel the ground sloping below his feet.

'Hey! It's going up.'

'Too true, mate, and look up there.'

Far above their heads, at the top of a kind of chimney, was daylight.

'Another way out,' shouted Tom, excited.

'Yeah, and you know what? We go out that way and they'll think we're still under here. What d'you reckon?'

'Smashing!' Then Tom stopped. 'How do we get up, though? It's too high.'

'We do like the steeplejacks. Put your back on one side and your feet on the other and walk up. Watch.'

As Tom stared he saw, by the faint light above, Scouser, body bent double, working his way up the chimney. Soon his climbing form blocked out the day.

'Come on,' his muffled voice commanded. Tom followed, heaving and straining with back and feet, spitting out the dirt that Scouser's boots showered on him.

Tom's whole body ached but he did not dare relax his knees. If he lost his grip he'd shoot right down into the tunnel again. Instead he pushed with all his might, shoulders, elbows, heels and toes.

'Here we are, kidder,' called Scouser.

Panting, they struggled out of the narrow opening into full daylight, blinking in the sun. Bushes blocked their way, but they shoved them to one side and stood up straight.

To look full into the muzzle of a rifle.

15

BEHIND THE GUN barrel loomed the sunburnt face and broad shoulders of a man in uniform.

As Tom and Scouser shot their hands into the air he burst into laughter.

'Stone the crows. A couple of kids.' He shouted over his shoulder. 'Hey, Corp!'

Tom and Scouser lowered their arms and gazed about them. They had climbed out at the top of the Clough, bang in the middle of the ack-ack emplacement. In front of them the grey gun barrel reached skywards, ringed in with neat rows of sandbags.

Further off, by the barbed wire, a fire was blazing. Two men in khaki were busy with a kettle. One turned and strode towards them. Tom recognized him by the two stripes on his sleeves.

'How did you two get in here?'

'Climbed up the pipe, mister. Hey, that's a smashing cannon. What sort is it?'

'Shouldn't really tell you, son,' said the bombardier sternly. But his eyes smiled. 'Still, Adolf knows all about these guns already. It's a Bofors 40 millimetre.'

Tom stared at the soldier's cap with its worn polished badge. He read the word 'Ubique'.

'Hey, my dad's got a badge like that,' he gasped. 'He was a bombardier in the last war.'

'Was he? I bet he saw some action,' the soldier said.

Scouser broke in. 'Not much action this time, eh, mister? Nothing happening.'

The bombardier looked serious. 'Don't kid yourself, son. This war's going to warm up before long.'

He pointed towards the gate in the barbed wire. 'And you two had better hop it before my battery commander comes. We'll be test-firing the gun soon. Hey, and don't come up the chimney again. That way's *verboten*.'

'OK!' Tom and Scouser spoke together. At the gate they turned and gave the thumbs-up sign.

Turning back, they stared into the baffled, angry face of William.

16

BEHIND WILLIAM STOOD Molly and Duggie, grinning with relief, and behind them Scouser's mates, open-mouthed.

'How did you get here?' demanded William. 'We've been looking all over the shop for you. We nearly went to the police.'

His voice stirred Tom's anger, which had been building up all week.

'Who are you trying to kid? You lot were playing cobs while Scouser and me were stuck down in the Caves.'

'Down in the Caves? You never. You both sneaked off out.'

Scouser stepped forward so aggressively that William moved back. He pointed to the mud on his jacket and Tom's.

'If we weren't down there, what's this stuff? Scotch mist?'

The others laughed, heating William up even more.

'Well, if you were in the Caves, how come you're up here now?' he asked furiously.

'That's a military secret,' answered Tom scornfully. 'Take no notice of him, Scouser.'

'You're finished in this gang,' William told Tom.

'No, he's not,' Molly spoke from behind William. 'He's still in, and so's Scouser if he wants, and his mates.'

'Who says?'

'I say,' piped up Duggie.

Scouser put his arm over Tom's shoulder. 'Come on, kidder,' he said. The gang, now enlarged, strolled towards home. William, after a pause to sulk, trailed after them.

Tom felt a warm glow spread inside him. Everything had turned out OK, after all.

But it hadn't.

17

JUST AS THE procession reached Tom's street it ran into an ambush. Widow Robertson, arms folded, stood in their path.

'Where have you been?' she demanded of Scouser. She stared. 'And all that filth on your windcheater.'

She turned on Tom. 'It's your fault. Taking him down one of your mucky places in his clean clothes.'

She raised her voice and the street rang.

'Wait till I tell your father.'

At these words, the little crowd split up like magic, each heading in a different direction. Tom was suddenly on his own.

With Widow Robertson's words in his ears, he crept up the garden path to his kitchen door.

But Tom's luck had not run out. Just as his unwilling foot was on the doorstep, a strange sound filled the air. It was a great wavering musical howl, rising and falling.

Dad appeared in the kitchen with Tom's little brother by the hand and carrying three gas-mask cases.

'About turn, son. Down to the shelter. That's the air-raid siren.'

Outside, now, the street was full of people, not hurrying but moving purposefully, smiling and joking, calling to one another.

Tom remembered the bombardier's words:

'It's going to warm up soon.' Was this it? Was Daneford going to be bombed flat?

At the top of the shelter steps stood William's dad, in a dark greatcoat and steel helmet.

'Take your places, please,' he called. 'There is no need to be alarmed. Everything is under control.'

The underground chamber was cold and

damp. It smelt of earth, and Tom was suddenly reminded of the Caves. Lights came on as people shuffled along the narrow benches, making room for each other.

Tom saw Molly on the seat opposite. She winked at him. He handed over her torch and whispered: 'The bulb went in the caves, sorry.'

She grinned. 'Forget it. It was worth it. The look on William's face, when he saw you and Scouser with those soldiers!'

As the shelter filled up, William's dad called, 'Everyone in now. The doors can be closed. Nothing to worry about. This may well be a false alarm.'

Just as he spoke there was a distant thud. The lights dimmed and a baby wailed. Someone called, 'Oh, they're dropping bombs.'

'No, no, love,' said Tom's dad. 'That's not a bomb. It's a gun, maybe that one at the Rec.'

As he spoke there came another 'crump'. William's dad spoke, importantly. 'That sounds too big for a gun.'

'It's a new sort of gun,' burst out Tom. 'A Bofors 40 millimetre. They're test-firing it.'

In the silence, everyone looked, amazed, at Tom. Dad grinned.

Then, as Tom swelled with pride, his mother said, 'Tom, what's that dirt on your sleeve?'

Tom gulped. But across the shelter, Widow

Robertson spoke soothingly. 'Oh, he probably picked it up in the shelter. Mucky places. My boy's got some on his windcheater.'

She patted Scouser's head. He made a face. Then she went on: 'I expect it'll all come out in the wash.'

Further along the benches, someone began to sing:

> *'We're going to hang out the washing*
> *on the Siegfried Line,*
> *Have you any dirty washing, Mother dear?'*

As the singing filled the shelter, from outside came another, louder sound, like the air-raid warning, but on one steady note.

'The all-clear, ladies and gentlemen,' said William's dad, getting in the last word.

Tom's War Patrol

ILLUSTRATED BY
STEPHEN PLAYER

1

'YOU, TOM! GET up now!' Tom was half awake. The tip of his nose was frozen, but under the blankets the rest of him was warm as toast. It was Saturday, so why was Mum shouting?

'Come on down, lad!'

There was no arguing with that voice. Reluctantly, he slid out of bed. The floor was cold. In his cot, close by, little brother Sam slept on.

'You, Tom, hurry up. Your 'vaccie friend's waiting in the back yard.'

That was funny, thought Tom, as he struggled, shivering, into his clothes. Scouser, the evacuee boy from Liverpool, had been his mate ever since he arrived in Daneford, just after the war started. It hadn't been easy at first. He and Scouser had fought in the schoolyard. But, in the end, Scouser had joined the Orchard Road gang.

The funny thing was, Scouser never called for him. They always met in the street.

As he stumbled downstairs, Tom peered through the side window. Snow had come down in the night. The whole world – ground, houses and sky – was shining white.

He hurried through the kitchen and opened the back door. A freezing blast of air made the kitchen fire flare up. Mum called out and Tom hastily closed the door behind him.

''Lo, Scouser. How're you blowing?' he began. Then he stopped, mouth half open.

Scouser stood, thin and pale, in the tiny snow-filled yard. He was wearing his Sunday best – well, someone else's Sunday best cast-off

and cut down. The words came into Tom's mouth: 'I bet those trousers are tight under the armpits.' But he said nothing, stopped by the look in Scouser's eye and the sight of the cardboard suitcase Scouser was carrying.

'I'm off wom,' said the Liverpool lad.

'What, for a weekend trip?' asked Tom.

'Nah. For good!'

Tom gasped. 'You're kidding. What about the air raids? I thought you came here 'cause it wasn't safe in Liverpool.'

Scouser looked disgusted. 'Air raids? There won't be any. This isn't a real war. They're just messing about.'

From inside the kitchen, Mum called out: 'Bring your friend in if you're going to talk. You'll both starve out there.'

Reluctantly Scouser was brought in and sat at the kitchen table. His eye caught the sight of Tom's breakfast – the rasher and slice of fried bread – and he looked quickly away. Mum cut the crust off the loaf, spread it thickly with margarine and offered it to him.

'It's all right, Missis. I've got my snap,' he said.

'Oh, you keep that for the bus, love,' answered Mum. Then she watched him eat. 'What's up, lad, don't you like it here?' she asked.

He shook his head. 'Nah. They're a pack of snobs. They only took us for the money. Some of my mates are sleeping three in a bed.'

Mum shook her head. 'Mrs Robertson didn't treat you like that, did she, lad?'

Scouser nodded. 'No, she's different. She's OK.'

He finished chewing and stood up. 'I'd better be off. The chara's waiting by the Co-op.'

Tom looked quickly at his mum. 'Shall I walk down the road with you?' He grabbed his coat from behind the door and they set off, trudging up Orchard Road in silence, the snow halfway up their boots. At the corner of Farm Lane, Scouser stopped and stuck out his hand. He clearly did not want Tom to come any further.

'Ta-ra well,' he muttered.

Tom shook Scouser's hand. He wanted to say, 'Shall we write?' but instead he just said: 'Ta-ra well.'

They parted, Scouser clumping along Farm Lane and Tom turning back down Orchard Road. He'd miss Scouser. But what was going to happen to him and the other Liverpool lads?

These thoughts were driven out of his head when something soft and wet hit the back of his neck. He swung round. There were the rest of the gang – William, Duggie and Molly – laughing and pointing.

Tom stopped, scooped up snow and hurled it back. The snowfight shifted down Orchard Road to the open space at the bottom. There the Barker's Crescent gang joined in and the battle grew fast and furious. But in the end Orchard Road drove the rival gang back into their own road and celebrated the victory by building a big snowman right in the middle of the open space, his stick nose pointing insolently into enemy territory. In the thick of the fight, Tom kept looking round half-expecting to see Scouser. But he was gone.

At tea time, all the family was round the table and, as Tom was spreading a piece of bread, his mother said sharply: 'Go careful with that. You know it's rationed, don't you?'

'That's right.' His dad laughed. 'Scrape it on and scrape it off again.'

Mum snapped, 'You can joke. But I have to make ends meet.'

'All right, love,' said Dad, soothingly.

Tom caught his mum's eye. She looked away.

He remembered her piling the margarine on to Scouser's crust this morning. It was almost as though she were sorry for the Liverpool lad.

But why? Nothing was going to happen to him, was it?

2

NEXT DAY MORE snow fell, and the next. The ponds were solid with ice. Winter 1940 was long and hard, the worst for forty years, said the wireless announcer.

Classes were half empty at school. But every day the school bus still slithered down the hill on a surface strewn with crushed rock salt. Hopes that the school might close were in vain.

Yet, weekends always came. Then there was snowballing, sliding on the ice, plunging down Jack's Hill on a sledge Duggie's dad knocked together from old boxes.

As Tom roamed and fought with his Orchard Road mates, his mind kept turning to Scouser. Why did he want to be there, in the dark back streets under the shadow of the docks in Liverpool? Still, that was home to him, wasn't it?

Tom missed Scouser in class. His whispered jokes and funny comments on what Teacher said had sent Tom into fits of suppressed laughter.

Tom missed Scouser out with the gang. The Liverpool lad had fitted in, though he was still an outsider, a townie. He was daring, taking risks that even impressed William, climbing and hurling himself from branches, across streams, landing with a swear word and a grin on his pale face.

Now he was gone, back to Liverpool, to some distant place where the war was. It all seemed unreal.

One weekend, Mum told Tom: 'You're to stop in this afternoon.'

Tom made a face. 'I'll have to miss Sunday School then,' he said slyly.

'You mean you'll have to miss snowballing. No, you're to stay in and put your new jumper on. Auntie Do and Archie are coming.'

Aunt Dorothea was posh. At least, she'd picked up posh notions as a housemaid, wore a fox fur and smoked scented cigarettes, scattering the ash and once leaving a burn mark on the arm rest of Dad's chair. Dad laughed it off. Mum didn't.

Archie was different. Archie was Tom's favourite cousin. His big sisters liked Archie too. Everyone did. He was sixteen, big, red-headed, a bit wild but always cheerful.

'Smashing,' said Tom.

But he was disappointed. Aunt Do came, fox fur, cigarettes and all, but no Archie. She threw herself down in Dad's armchair and looked at their questioning faces.

'I let our Archie go,' she said.

'Oh, Do!' Mum spoke reproachfully. 'You mean . . .?'

Aunt Do waved a long finger. 'Yes. He was

mad to join the fusiliers, like his grandad.'

'But they won't have him. He's too young,'
Mum protested.

'Almost seventeen. He put the rest on.' Aunt
Do paused. 'I gave him a letter for the
Recruiting Office, said we didn't have his birth
certificate. They were quite happy with that.'

'I bet they were,' murmured Dad. 'But what
does your Jack say?'

Aunt Do looked up at the ceiling. 'My Jack's never here when he's needed. I have to make my own mind up.'

'Where's Archie posted then?' asked Dad.

Aunt Do shrugged. 'Somewhere in England.'

'He's so young,' insisted Mum.

'Oh, he's got his head screwed on,' said Aunt Do carelessly. 'Anyway, he can't come to any harm, can he?' She looked at Dad. 'I mean, there's not going to be any real fighting. The papers are calling it the phoney war, aren't they?'

Everyone was silent over tea, though now and then Mum looked at her sister as though she would like to say something.

As she left, Aunt Do was smiling. She said, 'Well, now they're both out of the house I can start work at the munitions factory and make a bit of spending money.'

When she'd gone, Dad shook his head.

'She's a cool customer, your sister.'

Mum answered, 'Underneath, she's worried sick. I'd be.'

That night in bed, Tom thought about Archie. He pictured him in his fusilier's uniform 'somewhere in England'. Somehow the picture became merged with the pale face of Scouser, back in Liverpool, beneath the circle of barrage balloons, waiting for the air raids to begin.

He crept out of bed and peered through the side window. More snow had fallen. There was no moon, the world was still, only a lone truck climbing the valley with its masked headlights like a glow-worm in the dark.

Scouser was gone. Archie was gone. What would happen now?

3

ICE CRACKED AND snow melted at last. Spring and sunshine came again. The Orchard Road gang were back in their favourite hideout, the old oak tree at the end of the Common.

But their mood was sombre. The distant, unreal war had suddenly loomed closer; menacing.

Duggie, who always picked the higher branches, lay back balanced on a bough,

talking quietly, counting on his fingers.

'Hitler's got Norway, Denmark, Holland and Belgium. And he's in France now . . .'

'Right,' said Tom. 'Our Archie's out in France.' He saw his cousin in his imagination, broad-shouldered, red-haired, in battle-stained khaki, charging with rifle and bayonet.

William's voice broke in sharply: 'Jerry can't keep up this pace. Stands to reason. Our troops are just waiting for the right moment. Then they do a pincer movement, cut off Jerry's advance guard and counter-attack.'

Waving his arms violently, William went on: 'Anyway, old Chamberlain's out now. Churchill's taken over. He's in charge. You watch.'

Tom had heard the new war leader's gravelly voice over the wireless: '. . . nothing to offer, but blood, toil, tears and sweat'. It all sounded thrilling, but it didn't sound as though we were winning.

'My dad's been looking at France in my school atlas. He reckons our troops and the French are pulling back . . .' Tom began.

William came back furiously: 'Your dad only knows about the last war. My dad says British troops are pushing Jerry back at . .' William couldn't remember the name of the French town, but he glared triumphantly at Tom.

Molly looked at them. 'If you lot are going to have a row, I'm off.'

She slid down from her branch and swung to the grass below. Tom, glad of an excuse to break off the argument, climbed down after her. William and Duggie followed and the gang straggled back to Orchard Road. But William's voice was still raised, though Duggie was not answering.

As they drifted up the road to Tom's house,

they saw William's father, the air-raid warden, talking excitedly to Tom's dad. His voice reached the gang quite clearly.

'I'm sorry to say it, but you were right, Harold. Our troops are pulling out of France. I heard on the wireless just now. They're sending all the boats they can find – anything from ferries to cabin cruisers – to evacuate our lads from a place called Dunkirk.'

He paused then went on: 'It'll be a miracle if they get back.'

Tom turned to look at William, but his frowning face was turned away.

4

THE ORCHARD ROAD gang were roaming the countryside, amazed at what they saw. Huge timber hurdles and piled-up bales of hay dotted the Common, turning it into an obstacle course.

'That's to stop German troop transports landing,' said William.

Concrete cylinders lay in ditches along the country lanes.

'Tank traps,' explained William.

At the crossroads, all the signposts had been uprooted and carted away.

'That's so German paratroopers can't find their way.'

Duggie shook his head. 'D'you reckon Hitler's really going to invade?'

'Forced to,' answered William. 'Didn't you hear Churchill on the wireless?' He imitated the famous growl: 'We will fight them on the beaches, we will fight them in the streets; we shall never surrender.'

More surprises waited when they topped the rise by Borley Wood and looked down across the parkland.

Every square yard of grass was covered with men in khaki, sitting or lying down in the sun. As the gang came up to the park fence, Tom thought it looked like a battlefield. These men were exhausted, unshaven. Some were fast asleep.

Molly whispered, 'They must be back from France.'

Three soldiers stood near the fence, battledress tunics open, showing grubby vests. They looked dazed. Impulsively Molly offered a bag of sweets. Smiling tiredly they took one each.

'Back from Dunkirk?' asked William.

They eyed him for a moment, then one said, 'Just about, son.'

Another laughed, lip curled. 'We'd have been back sooner, only our captain took the unit truck and scarpered on his own.'

The first speaker, an older man, turned. 'You shut up. These kids don't need to know about that.'

'Will you be staying for a rest?' asked Molly.

All three laughed. 'Couple of days.'

'Where will you go?' asked William.

'If we knew, son, we couldn't tell you.'

'My cousin was in France,' Tom told them, 'in the fusiliers.'

One soldier shook his head. 'They were further south, son, don't know if they got away.'

Duggie butted in. 'Do you reckon Hitler's going to invade?'

'Haven't a clue, son.' The response was weary.

Now William raised his voice and the rest of the gang heard him in astonishment. 'We're going to form a junior LDV patrol. If there's an invasion we'll go out looking for German parachutists.'

The three men listened to him in silence, but behind them a sneering voice rose. 'Who're you kidding, Harris?'

Near by stood Hicks from Barker's Crescent, lean and foxy, with his ginger-headed sister Edith and their fat, fair-haired friend, Cissie Perkins.

'Anyway,' went on Hicksie, 'it's not LDV any more, it's Home Guard. My dad's joined. He's got a twelve-bore shotgun. Your dad can't join –' he poked a finger at William – 'he's just an air-raid warden.' Pointing at Tom, 'His dad's an ambulance man,' and with a curl of the lip at Duggie, 'his dad's always on shift work.'

Turning his back on the soldiers and facing the Barker's Crescent people, William furiously declared, 'We're forming a patrol, anyhow.'

'Pull the other,' jeered Hicksie. The girls beside him shrieked with laughter. Abruptly William jerked away, followed by the Orchard Road gang.

They tailed back to Daneford and home. William stalked ahead, pulling Duggie with him, arguing, arms waving. Tom heard him say, 'We'll show 'em.' And he knew somehow it was Barker's Crescent rather than the Germans William was talking about. But what was William plotting?

Molly's quiet voice broke into his thoughts. 'Our William gets so worked up.'

Tom looked at her. 'Well, Hicksie's rotten.'

Molly shook her head. 'Not as bad as his sister.'

Tom stared.

'She eggs him on. You don't know, Tom. Girls can be a lot worse than boys.'

As if reading his thoughts, she moved closer

to Tom and said, almost in a whisper, 'Put your leg in bed, Tom?'

He looked round. She chuckled. 'There's nobody.'

Tom slipped his arm into hers and she squeezed it. They walked home in companionable silence.

5

O N A BRIGHT summer Saturday, the
Orchard Road patrol set out on its
first recce. The arching blue sky was
crisscrossed with vapour trails and at home
the wireless buzzed with news of 'dog fights'
in the air.

William insisted on marching right down the
street and across the open ground by Barker's
Crescent on the way to the Common. He
went first, air gun slung across his chest. Tom

followed with a scout pole over his shoulder.
Duggie, sporting a large catapult, and Molly,
with a freshly tacked Red Cross armband
round her sleeve, brought up the rear.

Tom gritted his teeth, hoping they could move swiftly and quietly past enemy territory. But William insisted on shouting commands to his troops. To Tom's relief Barker's Crescent was empty. That ought to have warned him that something was brewing.

But as they climbed the stile and turned along the hedge that bordered the Common, his ears picked up small sounds – whispers, sniggers. If William heard them he ignored them and marched ahead, calling: 'Right, patrol! Keep your eyes peeled for bandits overhead. Watch out for parachutists coming down.'

At his words, the sniggers burst into raucous laughter and over the hedge came a shower of clods. Barker's Crescent was in ambush.

'Stand your ground, Orchard Road,' yelled William as he took one clump of earth from the side of his head. But the clods were followed by stones and Orchard Road was not looking for medals. In seconds the patrol was in full flight along the Common, speeded by the mocking laughter from beyond the hedge. It was a rout.

But if Tom, or Barker's Crescent, thought that William would give up, they were much mistaken.

Next Friday night a scribbled note was pushed through the front door at Tom's:

Private Taylor: Report to Private Barnes' shed, 0900 hours tomorrow. Bring scout knife. Signed Sergeant Harris.

Tom found the rest of the patrol crowded into the tiny shed at the back of Duggie's garden. William was beaming.

'Look at that,' he crowed.

Across the workbench used by Duggie's father, lay three rifles with webbing straps. Tom gasped. 'Where d'you get those?'

Duggie grinned proudly. 'They're just

wood, painted. Dad's doing a lot for the Home Guard drill practice. He made these extra for us – just a bit smaller.'

'Get a load of this,' said William impatiently. He held up four khaki forage caps. 'Dad got them from a bloke at the depot.'

Tom turned to Molly. She carried a brown haversack stamped with a Red Cross.

'Now,' said William, handing out the rifles, 'see the slot under the barrel. You fit your scout knife in there. We're parading with fixed bayonets today.'

This time, the patrol marched down Orchard Road, past Barker's Crescent and on to the Common in silence, save for William's barked commands. They were watched, Tom knew, but this time there was no mocking laughter and no shower of grass clumps.

William had other ideas too. At the end of the Common stood an old oak tree with low, spreading branches, where the gang often met. From one of these branches hung a strange object, like a Guy Fawkes, a grey jacket stuffed with straw and held together with a leather belt.

'Patrol, halt!' commanded William. 'First Aid section fall out. Combatants present arms.' He pointed to the dark shape swinging from the branch. 'Now that is an enemy parachutist caught in a tree.'

Levelling his rifle with its projecting knife blade, he let out a howl and charged at the swinging dummy. Plunging the 'bayonet' deep into the 'parachutist', he dragged it out and turned back triumphantly.

'Private Barnes. At the double!'

Duggie followed, then Tom. At first they stumbled awkwardly. But soon the excitement gripped them. Tom ran, thrust, yelled along with the rest and in his mind's eye he saw Archie, still fighting his rearguard action over in France.

'Get 'em, patrol!' bellowed William, until at

last, sweating and exhausted, they flung themselves on the grass. It was then that Tom noticed Molly was sitting some little way away, her back turned to them. But, when William gave the order, he jumped up with Duggie and the charging began again until the dummy was so slashed it had to be bound up with string.

By the time the exercise was over and the patrol equipment stored in Duggie's shed, Tom was late home for dinner. But his mother didn't seem to notice.

'What d'you think, Tom? Our Archie's safe after all.'

'D'you mean he's come back?'

'No, but Auntie Do had a letter to say he's in a PoW camp in Germany.'

'Hey,' said Tom, 'maybe he'll escape and get back into action again.'

His mother retorted: 'I hope not. At least he's safe there till the end of the war.'

Tom was about to protest, but something in his mother's eye made him keep quiet.

6

NEXT SATURDAY, TOM was on his way out to join the patrol when Mum called him back.

'Tom. Take a bucket, will you, and get off up to Hundred Acre. They're clearing the top field for a supply dump. Farmer's letting everybody pick their own spuds, free.'

'Smashing,' said Tom. 'I'll take two buckets.'

'No, you won't, love. One bucket each.

That's the ration. Off you go. I expect they'll all be up there.'

So they were. The huge field was swarming with people, young and old, while tractors hauling diggers circled round throwing out black earth and white potatoes.

Orchard Road was there and so was Barker's Crescent. The two gangs eyed one another warily, buckets in hand.

With a roar and a pungent cloud of diesel fumes, the tractor chugged along the drill, digger wheels spinning, potatoes flying. Everyone jumped clear, then as the machine passed they ran with their buckets.

Suddenly the tractor jerked to a shuddering halt, belching black smoke. A trim figure in broad-brimmed hat, brown shirt and breeches leapt from the driver's seat, rushed at the digger shouting strange words and kicking the wheels.

As both gangs, open-mouthed, drew near, the driver turned a sunburnt face with bright brown eyes on them. 'What's the matter? Never seen a woman drive a tractor?'

The voice was accented. She glared, they stared. Then Hicksie said, 'Hey, you're not English.'

For a moment she eyed them defiantly, then answered, 'No, I'm not, I'm German.'

Gathered in a circle, they gaped at her.

'If you're German, what are you doing here?' demanded William. The driver frowned, was about to turn back to the stalled machine, then changed her mind. She came closer to them and spoke slowly.

'Because, although people over here don't seem to understand, not all Germans like Hitler. My brother and I escaped.'

'What about your mother and father?' asked Tom.

She spoke very quietly. 'My mother died. The Gestapo took my father.'

'Is he dead?' blurted William.

There was no answer and Molly hastily asked, 'What's your name?'

Now she smiled. 'Lieselotte. They call me Leelo.'

Molly went on. 'Maybe you'll see your dad again when the war's over.'

Leelo shrugged and bent over the digger wheel.

'Yeah,' added William. 'We're gonna beat Hitler. Spitfires are miles better than Messerschmitts, any day. They shot down sixty-nine the other day.'

Leelo looked up from the machine. 'You know, my brother wants to join the British Army to fight Hitler. They locked him up, just because he's German. He said to me, "You know, the British may just win, because they don't understand who they're fighting. They think it's all a big game." Hitler and the Nazis, you know, they'll destroy anyone, anywhere, who's against them – Germans as well.'

She gave a huge jerk. The digger wheel spun free. She leapt on to the tractor seat and the engine came to life. Potatoes began to spill on to the ground again.

As the gangs began to fill their buckets, Duggie burst into song. The others joined in.

'When Der Führer says, vee is der master race.

'We sing Heil, fart, Heil, right in the Führer's face.'

Tom looked up. Leelo had turned in her driving seat and was looking back at them, slowly shaking her head. But she was laughing.

7

SERGEANT HARRIS RAN his eye along the Orchard Road patrol. Assembly Point Number One – Duggie's shed – was dusty and hot in the morning sun. But William kept the troops at attention. He leant forward to straighten Tom's forage cap. It was really too big for him and had settled over his right eye. Then William stood back.

'You heard the news this morning. Another fifty-four Heinkels, Dorniers and

Messerschmitts downed yesterday. But we still have to keep on our toes.'

He might have said more, but Molly yawned and looked out of the window. Her cousin took the hint and quickly marched the patrol out into Orchard Road and down to the Common. These days there were no fixed bayonets. Widow Robertson had spotted them and made a fuss over 'waving knives about in the street'.

But once out on the Common and over to the oak tree where the 'parachutist' hung in its tattered grey jacket, William gave the order, 'Fix bayonets!'

Duggie and Tom joined in with gusto. Molly, as usual, sat some little way off, her first-aid kit on her knees, looking into the distance. But the lads, hot and sweating, excited with their rushing and jabbing, barely noticed.

An hour passed, then disaster struck. William,

howling his war cry 'Yaaaaah!', flung himself on the parachutist so furiously that the rifle and bayonet passed right through the dummy. The force of his charge carried William, target and all, in an upward swing. With a rending crash, the old bough gave way and collapsed on

William as he fell, still grappling with the enemy.

Duggie and Tom, aghast and spluttering with laughter at the same time, heard him cry out: 'First-aid team here. At the double.'

Slowly Molly got to her feet and walked over

to stand by the fallen Patrol Leader.

'There's nowt wrong with you, William, and you know it. Perhaps now you'll pack this stupid game in.' She looked at Tom and Duggie. 'You're a bloodthirsty lot, you know.'

William struggled up, red-faced. 'There's a war on, or hadn't you heard?'

Sarcasm was wasted on Molly. She retorted: 'I know there is. I'm not stupid. I listen to the wireless, the same as you do. I heard them say the Battle of Britain's over. Hitler's not coming any more.'

Saying that, she turned her back and walked away, leaving the rest of the patrol spread out on the grass.

But Molly was wrong.

That night, Tom woke to the crump of the anti-aircraft gun on the Rec and the wail of sirens. Dad was taking Sammy downstairs. He followed and joined the rest of the family in the darkened kitchen. Dad was peering through a chink in the blackout curtain.

'Are we going to the shelters, Dad?'

'No, lad. They're not after us. They're going over, heading west. Listen.'

High in the night sky, Tom's ear caught the wavering drone of German bombers – many of them.

Tom looked out through the gap in the curtains. To his astonishment, the sky in the west was rosy like a great sunset. The small black blobs of barrage balloons swung black against the red glare.

'What's that, Dad?'

'That's Liverpool brewing up, son. They're going to cop it tonight.'

When Tom got back into bed, he slept restlessly. His dreams were a mad jumble of falling bombs, people running and shouting

– Scouser, Archie, dark-eyed Leelo.

And swinging above them all was the grotesque giant shape of the 'parachutist'.

8

THE ORCHARD ROAD patrol was out of action. Molly had clearly given it the thumbs down, Duggie was busy on some money-making scheme of his father's. And William was nursing injuries, chiefly to his pride.

Tom was on his own, hanging about the house at weekends until his mother either drove him out on errands, or set him to turn the wheel of the mangle roller, while she did the endless washing.

This he didn't mind since from the washhouse he could hear the wireless bulletins, the clipped voice of the announcer: '. . . last night the Luftwaffe attacked the London docks. Southampton, Hull and Liverpool were also subjected to heavy raids . . . Our air force retaliated with raids over Hamburg and Dusseldorf . . .'

Tom listened as he turned the handle, while the white sheets squeezed through between the rollers and the soapy water poured into the tub below. His mother would say, 'I think I'll switch that off. It's nothing but raids, raids, raids.'

'Aw, Mum,' protested Tom, in vain.

At night he listened as the aircraft droned westwards towards Liverpool. By now he could clearly distinguish the up and down note of the German bombers from the more even

sound of the British planes.

Once he woke to the wavering engine sound to hear the roar as a night fighter dived, then the clatter of machine guns in the dark overhead. Sometimes the anti-aircraft gun on the Rec would open up and next day he would rush out into the streets hunting for jagged lumps of shrapnel.

The sirens would go. But nowadays no one went to the shelters. Dug too close to the river, they were ankle deep in water. And everyone knew – it's not for us, Liverpool's copping it.

One evening, Widow Robertson was at the back door with a letter.

'There's one for you, Tom.'

Tom took the single crumpled sheet with its pencilled scrawl to the bottom of the garden and sat under the hedge to read it. It was slow work.

...THEY CAME ROUND OUR WAY WITH ANDERSON SHELTERS. "PUT 'EM IN YOUR GARDEN," SAYS THIS BLOKE. MY DAD TOLD HIM, "GARDEN, WHAT GARDEN?"

SO, WHEN THE BOMBING STARTED, THERE WAS NOWHERE TO GO ROUND OUR WAY. SOME PEOPLE WENT RIGHT OUTSIDE IN THE FIELDS AND STAYED THERE ALL NIGHT.

MY DAD AND HIS MATES FROM THE DOCKS, THEY KICKED OPEN ONE OF THE BIG WAREHOUSE DOORS. EVERYBODY FROM ROUND OUR WAY WENT INTO THE BASEMENT. BUT ONLY FOR A FEW NIGHTS. THESE DAYS WE DON'T BOTHER. JUST GET UNDER THE KITCHEN TABLE AND LISTEN. I'D WATCH OUT OF THE WINDOW IF THEY'D LET ME.

IF YOU CAN HEAR THE BOMBS COMING DOWN YOU'RE OK. SOMEBODY ELSE HAS GOT IT. IF YOU DON'T HEAR THEM, YOU'VE HAD IT.

SEE YOU SOMETIME. YOUR OLD PAL, SCOUSER.

On impulse, Tom walked round to Molly's and showed her the letter. She read it and handed it back silently. But she smiled at Tom.

'Are you coming out on Saturday?' asked Tom.

'Don't mind, as long as you don't play that stupid charging game.'

Tom thought quickly. 'If William and Duggie aren't coming, shall we go out, ourselves?'

She turned slightly pink, then laughed, punched Tom on the shoulder and said, 'You're on.'

9

THROUGHOUT THAT RED–GOLD autumn, Tom and Molly roamed the countryside, exploring the streams and copses, climbing up to the moors. They lay on the sedge by the mere and listened to the drumming of the snipe in the hazy air, or watched the skylark flutter higher and higher. Once they looked over a bank to find three tawny fox cubs playing in the sand outside their earth. The war seemed far away.

Then, one winter's day, when the snow was like icing on a cake, they came to the parkland near Borley Wood. Nissen huts had been built beneath the trees. Men in maroon battle dress moved about beyond the barbed wire.

'Who are they?' whispered Molly.

Tom knew. 'They're Italian PoWs from Africa. Wavell's winning out there now.'

'What are those circles on their backs for?'

'So the guards can shoot at 'em if they run away.'

'That's cruel,' said Molly. Tom didn't answer.

As winter passed, war came closer again. More raids, heavier raids, across the country, graver news on the wireless. Random attacks came more often.

Just before dawn, Tom was plucked from his sleep by the whistle of bombs. Sammy let out a howl as the crash of the explosions shook the house. Tom lifted his little brother up and staggered downstairs with him. Dad was struggling into his jacket.

'Good lad, Tom. You're all right. Hit and run. I'm off down the road to see if anyone's hurt.' He hurried out, haversack over his shoulder.

No one was hurt. A stick of bombs had breached the canal bank and just missed the river locks. Daneford could talk of nothing else. London, Liverpool were forgotten, though that week the port was taking a terrible hammering.

Towards the end of the week, the word went round: 'The 'vaccies are coming back. They've had enough.'

That Saturday, Tom raced down to the garage. The coach was already there with the Liverpool kids, pale and grim, climbing down. Tom caught one lad by the sleeve, blurting out, 'Is Scouser with you?'

They looked at him suspiciously. One lad, bigger than the rest, moved closer. 'You trying to be funny, mate? We're all Scousers.'

Another put in, staring at Tom, 'I know who he means. He means Billie Doherty.'

There was a moment's deep silence. Then the

big lad said, 'Billie? He copped it last week, and his mum and dad. Land mine, flattened the street. They didn't stand a chance.'

They pushed past Tom, leaving him staring. One turned back and said quietly, 'That's it, mate.'

These sympathetic words made Tom's throat tighten. He gulped to clear it and began to walk aimlessly. After a while he found himself outside Molly's house. Maybe that was where he was heading, without thinking. But Molly was out, down in Castleton with her aunt. She'd be back at tea time.

Tom walked on into the country. The hedgerows were turning green. The sun was shining. But he trudged with his eyes on the ground, seeing only Scouser's pale features and sharp eyes and thinking, I'll never see him again. He's gone. Didn't stand a chance.

He pictured a row of small houses, roofs,

windows, kitchens, bedrooms, all turned into rubble. Try as he would he could not get the image out of his head.

Someone called: 'Hang on, Tom.'

Duggie and William were jog-trotting along behind him.

'Where're you off to? We kept shouting.' Duggie looked closely at him. 'What's up, Tom?'

Tom told them quickly, exactly as the Liverpool lads had told him.

'Poor old Scouser,' said Duggie.

William stood still in front of them. 'I vote we start the patrol again. Get one of them. Right?'

'Right,' said Duggie.

Tom nodded slowly.

10

THE ORCHARD ROAD patrol lay on the grass at the top of the Banks, the highest point above Daneford. Their rifles were stacked in a triangle behind them. Below, the fields and woods, now green again with spring, stretched away, eastwards to the smoke of the works chimneys, westwards towards the grey barrage balloons around Liverpool. Above them the sky was blue and empty as it had been for weeks now.

The patrol's searching seemed in vain.

Molly pulled daisies and began to thread them, despite her cousin's scowl. 'Honest, William,' she said, 'do you really think some German parachutist's going to drop out of the sky, right on top of us?'

'They only fly by night now,' added Duggie helpfully. 'They're scared of coming by day.'

William's mouth thinned. 'We can't let up. There's hit and run raids, sometimes they dump their bomb loads when our lads get on their tails. Then there's recce planes.'

He paused for effect. 'Over at Cullingham, two blokes on a farm caught a German pilot last week. They were going to stick a pikel in him, but the Home Guard came up and stopped them. Then, would you believe it, the farmer's wife made him a cup of tea,' he finished in disgust.

The conversation died and the patrol gazed

up at the empty sky in silence. Sometimes, thought Tom, the war seemed so far away, so unreal — tanks in the desert, convoys in the Atlantic, even bombs on Liverpool. Then he thought of Scouser, buried under the rubble, and Archie behind the barbed wire of a prison camp.

He could see their faces so clearly, and Leelo's with her dark eyes and cheeky grin. Yet they were all like part of a dream.

He almost wished a German plane would dive out of the blue, scattering parachutists like dandelion seeds.

But nothing happened. The sky stayed empty. The patrol grew hungry and tired of watching and they went home.

At tea time, Tom's mother brought him back to earth. 'Just you go easy with that jam, our Tom. That's the last you'll get till next month.'

The line between her eyes deepened. She

turned to one of Tom's older sisters and pointed to the plate. 'What can you do with an ounce of cheese each a week? What sort of a ration's that?'

Later that evening, Tom had finished his homework and went out into the kitchen for a quick wash before going up to bed. Through the open window he could hear his dad and Bert Harris, the air-raid warden, having one of their arguments down by the gate.

'Well, Harold, we're all in the same boat,' said William's dad.

'Just about,' retorted Dad. 'But some are still travelling first class and the rest of us steerage. Look, Bert, you know very well that some people can buy what they want on the black market. They live the way they always did. They don't know there's a war on.'

Their voices drifted away down the street.

11

I T CAME WITHOUT warning, out of a clear
summer sky. The patrol was at ease, lying
on the edge of the old quarry, watching
the rabbits frisking on the turf in front of
their warren.

Like magic, the animals raised noses in the air,
froze for a second, then scattered to vanish into
the shelter of the bank.

A thin sound on the horizon spread to a
howling scream as two Spitfires, with curved

wings and green-brown camouflage, roared across, just above their heads, soared upwards and away into the distance.

The patrol held its breath as the sound died and like an echo drifted back the urgent 'da da da da da' of machine guns. Then nothing, the sky above was blue and empty once more.

'Hey,' whispered Duggie. 'They must have scrambled from Wansford base.'

'Hope they got 'em,' Tom muttered.

But emptiness and silence were the only answer. The patrol lay back. The rabbits began to poke heads out from the warren. There was a faint scent of flowers on the breeze.

And the sky at their backs opened to a roar like an express train out of control, that grew to a shriek that pierced the ears, closer and closer, louder and louder.

A huge shadow, a mighty wind, a terrible din, passed over them and their upraised eyes saw in a split second the grey plane with its black crosses fall down from the sky to vanish behind the rise just ahead. There was a rending crash then an awful silence.

'Come on,' yelled William. 'This is it!' And they were all racing to the top of the slope, to stop abruptly.

In the newly ploughed field below them, an enormous vee of twisted metal reared up, engines forming one arm, tail the other. The wings, torn off, lay crumpled to one side.

Duggie grabbed Tom's arm, pointing. 'There's one.' A lone figure pulled away from the plane and staggered towards them.

'Fix bayonets,' commanded William.

But no one heard, no one moved. A huge tongue of flame lapped up from the wreckage, a searing blast of air, solid as a wall, struck them. And the running figure, just down the slope, was burning too, shoulders, head and arms,

burning and screaming. Still alight, the figure
collapsed almost at their feet.

For a second they were paralysed with
horror. Then Molly leapt forward, tearing
off her jacket and beating at the flames,

pressing down the cloth on the tortured body. Tom was at her side as she lifted her scorched coat. He saw the blackened face of a young man, blue eyes staring.

'He's a goner,' said a voice behind them. Sergeant Collins from the police station, enormous, red-faced, leaning on his bike, looked down on their pale, up-turned faces.

'I followed this one down from the road,' he added. Dropping his bike, he bent over the body, reached out a hand and passed it slowly over the airman's face. Now the eyes stared no more.

Sergeant Collins handed Molly's jacket to her. 'Spoilt that, haven't you? Waste of time. Did you think you could save the bloke's life?'

Saying nothing, Molly took the jacket. Sergeant Collins looked the patrol over, noting the wooden rifles and smiled grimly. 'I'll wait for the Army. You lot had better get off home.'

None of them looked back as they made their way to the road. They did not need to, because inside the head of each one of them the film reeled slowly, crash, wreckage, flames, airman running, burning.

None of them spoke. They walked slowly, Molly turning her half-burnt jacket over and over in her hands. Tom stole quick glances at her, but could not meet her eye. It was as though he were seeing her for the first time. He could not grasp what she had just done.

At last, when they reached the Common, William broke the silence. Jerking his head towards the way they had come, he said: 'Let's not tell anyone what happened back there, eh? You know what I mean?' And as he spoke he gave his cousin a long look. 'There's no need for anyone else to know.'

But William was wrong, very wrong.

12

TOM SENSED TROUBLE as the four reached the stile that led from the Common. The entrance to Barker's Crescent was crowded. The Crescent gang lined the open ground that led into Orchard Road. Other kids were hanging about. Women, arms folded over aprons, stood by garden gates. And right at the front, faces shining with malice, were Edith Hicks and Cissie Perkins. As the patrol came over the stile, a muttering grew to a growl. Someone started to boo.

'Keep going,' ordered William. 'First one who tries anything, clout him with your rifle and run for our road.'

But first to move was Edith Hicks. Closely followed by Cissie, she planted herself in Molly's path and spat out: 'We know what you did. Uncle Joe was rabbiting up by the old quarry. He saw you trying to save that Jerry.' She looked round, then raised her voice.

'If you love 'em that much, why didn't you jump on the fire yourself.' She pushed her face into Molly's and poked a finger into her chest. 'We don't want your sort round here.'

It seemed Molly did not hear what Hicksie's sister was saying. She looked past Edith's flushed face to the crowd and raised her voice. 'You have no idea what you're talking about. You don't know anything.'

Slowly, firmly, she pushed Edith's prodding

finger aside. 'Excuse me –' she began.

'Don't you lay hands on me,' squealed Edith. She and Cissie sprang at Molly, grabbing clothes, snatching hair, hurling her to the ground. Tom started forward.

'Leave 'em,' snapped William. 'It's girls.'

'It's two on one,' protested Tom and without more thought launched himself on the struggling group, clutching at Edith's ginger hair and Cissie's neck band. It ripped away in his hand, but the force of his heave sent both attackers backwards.

Three things happened at once. Duggie ran forward to help Molly to her feet. Hicksie, swearing, aimed a ferocious kick at Tom's head. But before it could land, William threw all his frustration into a mighty swipe that brought blood jetting from Hicksie's nose.

'Run for it,' shouted William and they did, into Orchard Road. But the Crescent mob followed. All the rules were broken today.

A half brick caught Tom on the forehead as he looked back. His head exploded in pain. His knees gave way. But William held him up.

'We're nearly there, Tom,' he gasped.

Now the Barker's Crescent gang fell back as Widow Robertson swept like a tank from her gate, yard brush swinging.

'You lot, get back where you belong,' she ordered. 'And you, Charlie Moss, just throw another brick and I'll skin you like a rabbit. And you can tell your dad as well.'

With a final quelling glare at Barker's Crescent, she swept the four into the yard behind Tom's house. Pushing open the back door, she called: 'Mrs Taylor, your lad's been in the wars.'

13

IT SEEMED THE tiny kitchen was full of people, all talking at once. Ignoring them, Dad sat Tom down by the fire and opened his first-aid box. Tom felt the smooth swabbing of the cotton wool, then the bubble and sting of the peroxide and last the soft touch of lint and plaster.

Then he felt his mother push him gently up the stairs into the bedroom. She helped him undress and tucked him into bed.

'I'll be up later, love,' she told him.

Tom lay there, the late afternoon sun shining through the window. Slowly the dizziness began to fade and a powerful ache took its place. Downstairs, voices were raised. He heard Mrs Perkins' screech.

'Do you know what your lad did to our Cissie, Mr Taylor? Tried to pull her frock off and tore it. That's going to cost . . .'

And Widow Robertson's grating voice.

'Go on then, tell Mr Taylor what your Cissie did to Molly Carter. Tell him who started it. Who pushed her on the ground and plugged her hair, eh?'

Dad's deeper tones chimed in.

'Shall we all go in the front room and sit down. Then we can talk this over quietly. I'd very much like to know what it's all about.'

Voices faded as people filed into the front room. Now Tom could only hear a vague hum of conversation. Light in the window slowly faded. Little Sammy rushed into the bedroom followed swiftly by Mum.

'Now, you get into bed and go to sleep. Don't mither your brother. He's got enough on his plate.' Then to Tom: 'Your dad'll be up in a while, when he's found out what it's all about.'

She closed the door quietly behind her. Sam, after one or two attempts to get Tom's attention, turned his back and curled up in sleep. Tom was left to his aching head and the lump of misery in his stomach.

Strange, disturbing feelings were struggling inside him. Deep down was the horror of what he had seen – death, not on the wireless nor in the newsreels, not even in the story about Scouser, but real, close up, inescapable. Then, shock at the way Molly had rushed to help the German pilot, while he could not move – for fear?

And there was shame and anger, the cat-calls of the Barker's Crescent mob, and himself, scrapping on the ground with two girls.

And now, now that Dad had found out what happened, what was he going to say?

14

IT WAS DARK outside now. Mum had lit the small oil lamp on the mantelshelf and it cast an oval of light up the wall to the sloping ceiling. Tom watched it waver to and fro and gradually he felt himself dozing off.

A slight sound woke him. A great shadow filled the lamp light. Dad had silently entered the bedroom and was sitting on the side of the bed looking at him. Tom forced his eyes to meet Dad's.

'You awake, Tom?'

'Ye-es.'

'Right. Well, just you tell me what happened. Don't worry about our Sam. You could drive a truck through here and not wake him.'

He listened while Tom relived the events of the day – the tongue of flame, the wall of heat, the young airman screaming and his blue eyes staring at the sky. Then the crowd, the insults and the scrambling in the dust.

There was a long, long pause, then Dad said, 'Well, do you think Molly did the right thing?'

Tom gulped. What could he say? Had he gone to Molly's rescue because he thought she did the right thing trying to save the German, or was it just because she was Molly? Or was it really because he was angry with Barker's Crescent, angry with everything, things he was afraid of but couldn't escape? 'I don't know,' he admitted, at last.

Dad nodded. 'Well, think on. You're just starting to find out what war's about.'

For a moment Dad seemed to be looking into the far distance. Then he said: 'Killing blokes is only one part of war, you know. If it were that simple I've killed enough Germans to last this family, blew 'em to pieces at five

hundred, one thousand feet range. And they did the same to our lads. And what difference did it make?'

Dad nodded as if to himself, and went on.

'In the last lot, we knew what war was like, all right. The trouble was we didn't know what it was about. When we came home after the war,

they promised us we'd have homes fit for heroes. And we said, "You'd have to be heroes to live in 'em."

'So, it's got to be different this time round. What matters in a war is what happens afterwards. Are things going to be better? So think on, son.'

Dad rose. His shadow leapt in the lamplight. He bent and ruffled Tom's hair.

Tom whispered: 'Do you think there'll be a raid tonight, Dad?'

Dad shook his head. 'No bomber moon, lad. It's black as Old Nick's waistcoat out there. Go to sleep.'

The bedroom door closed. Tom lay still, listening. Down in the valley, the bells of the shunting engines clanged faintly.

From far above came the sound of an aircraft. Tom half sat up. It was a steady, droning note. One of ours.

He sank back on the pillow and a moment later he was fast asleep.